For Mila and Kate -

my everything now and always.

She Is

Written by Mandie Frey

Illustrated by Laura Catrinella

She is *my everything*, wrapped into one.

She is *laughter*,
bundled with fun.

She is *beauty*... a heart so full and bright.

She is *sunshine*, showering the world with light.

She is *happiness*,
spreading joy all day.

She is *grace*, sharing love along her way.

She is *adventure*, exploring high and low.

She is *vibrant* ...
a wildflower eager to grow.

She is *curiosity* ... an ever-questioning mind.

She is *friendship*, loyal, honest, and kind.

FACULTY OF EDUCATION

She is *brilliance*,
reaching for the sky.

She is *courage* ...
no summit is too high.

She is *hope*, softening others' sorrow.

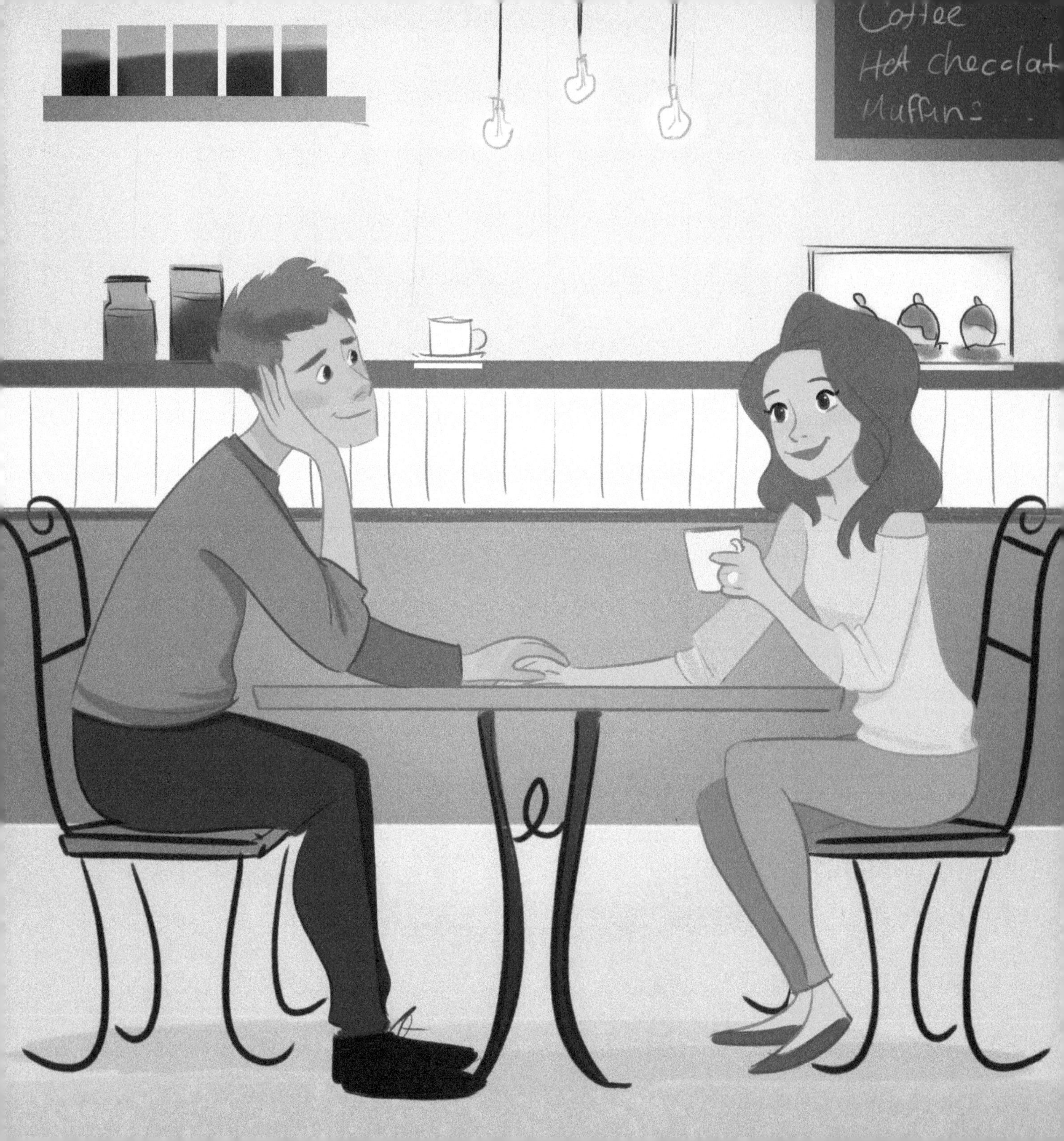
Coffee
Hot chocolat
Muffins . . .

She is *trust* ... a promise for tomorrow.

She is *worthy* of life's greatest treasure.

She is
my daughter,
loved beyond measure.

Mandie Frey

is an elementary school teacher and a mother to two young daughters. When she is not adventuring with her kids or wondering where to travel next, she is dreaming of what will inspire her pen to hit the paper. Frey lives in Strathcona County, Alberta with her husband, Colten, and their wonderful daughters, Mila and Kate. The family also includes a much-loved beagle, Ovie.

FriesenPress

Suite 300 - 990 Fort St
Victoria, BC, V8V 3K2
Canada

www.friesenpress.com

Illustrated by Laura Catrinella

ISBN
978-1-5255-5679-1 (Hardcover)
978-1-5255-5680-7 (Paperback)
978-1-5255-5681-4 (eBook)

1. Juvenile Fiction, Family,
New Baby

Distributed to the trade by The
Ingram Book Company

CPSIA information can be obtained
at www.ICGtesting.com
Printed in the USA
BVHW020340061120
592666BV00001B/7

9 781525 556791